P9-ASD-262

As I open this book,

I remember that I am a child of God,

A follower of Jesus who walks in his way of love.

Dear Jesus, help me use my gifts

To pray for others,

To work for justice and peace,

And to help those in need,

So that I can serve the Kingdom of God

With my own two feet of love in action.

Amen.

Ouahigouya

Kaya

Koudougou

OUAGADOUGOU

Diapaga

BURKINA FASO

Bobo-Dioulasso

Banfo

Sylvie's village

GHANA

TOGO

CÔTE D'IVOIRE

BURKINA FASO

Drop by Drop

**United States Conference of Catholic Bishops,
Department of Justice, Peace, and Human Development**

In Partnership with Loyola Press

Illustrated by Carrie Gowran

LOYOLAPRESS.
A JESUIT MINISTRY

Schoharie Free Library
103 Knower Ave
PO Box 519
Schoharie, NY 12157

LOYOLAPRESS.
A JESUIT MINISTRY

3441 N. Ashland Avenue
Chicago, Illinois 60657
(800) 621-1008
www.loyolapress.com

Text © 2015 United States Conference of Catholic Bishops

Illustrations © 2015 Loyola Press

All rights reserved.

Author: United States Conference of Catholic Bishops;
Department of Justice, Peace, and Human Development

Contributing Editor: Susan Blackaby

Cover design: Carrie Gowran

Illustrations: Carrie Gowran

ISBN-13: 978-0-8294-4100-0

ISBN-10: 0-8294-4100-X

Library of Congress Control Number: 2014959765

Printed in the United States of America.

18 19 20 Bang 10 9 8 7 6 5 4 3 2

Sister Mary Jerome has a nephew named Mike. He works for Catholic Relief Services in West Africa. He has been living in a small country called Burkina Faso. He visited our class to tell us about his experiences.

Mike started by asking us to name the chores we do to help our families. We told him how we pitch in, and Mike made a list.

Then Mike showed us a picture of a girl carrying a big jug of water on her head.

"This is my friend, Sylvie," said Mike. "She is about your age. Girls like Sylvie have an important job. Every day they collect the water their family needs. I'm going to tell you about Sylvie and the Water Project that made her dream come true . . ."

Chores We Do

Clean up my room.

Set the table.

Rake leaves.

Take out the trash.

Walk the dog.

Sylvie's Story

Sylvie woke up early and stretched. She could tell it would be a hot day. She imagined the wind blowing across the Sahara Desert to her little village in Burkina Faso. She wanted to stay in the cool, dark house. But she needed to get going.

"Sylvie!" called her older sister, Flora. "Come and eat!"

8

"Hurry up!" said her oldest sister, Marie. "We won't wait for you if you are late!"

Breakfast was ready. They all sat down to eat before they went to work. Papa and Sylvie's older brother, Jean, had to go to the fields. Mama had to gather wood and tend the fire. Grandmother had to watch the baby. Sylvie's younger brother, Felix, had to go to school.

9

Sylvie wanted to go to school with Felix, but she had to go with her sisters instead. Sylvie had to fetch the family's water.

Sylvie put on her flip-flops. She picked up her empty jug and followed her sisters up the path. The river was a three-mile walk from the village.

Sylvie trudged up the path, counting her steps. Sometimes she counted by twos. Sometimes she counted by tens. As the sun rose higher, Sylvie imagined sitting in the schoolroom beside Felix. Thinking about letters, words, numbers, and sums helped her pass the time.

At the river, Sylvie splashed and played with Flora and Marie. The water felt good on her hot feet. She rested on a big rock in the shade. Then she filled her water jug. She lifted it up high and set it on her head. She began the slow walk home.

12

The sun was low in the sky when Sylvie got back to the village. Felix ran out to meet her. He took the water jug from her.

"Sylvie, come see!" he said. "Mr. Mike has a surprise for you!"

Sylvie rubbed her stiff neck. "What are you talking about?" she said.

Then Sylvie saw it, parked beside her home. It was a small cart that held four big plastic jugs.

"The cart will help you carry water from the river," said Felix. "No more jugs to lug."

Sylvie touched the cart handle. She smiled. The cart would make the trip much faster. Could she get back from the river in time to go to school? She could try!

The next morning the girls headed out of the village. Sylvie pulled the water cart.

Felix trotted along beside her as far as the school.

"Hurry back!" he said. "I'll save you a seat."

15

Sylvie waved to Jean in the fields. Jean pointed and teased. "Look at the little donkey pulling her cart!" he said.

Sylvie grinned. "Hee haw!" she said.

She hopped and kicked. She felt happy as the cart bumped behind her on the path.

At the river, Sylvie worked fast. Flora and
Marie splashed while Sylvie filled each jug.
They played while Sylvie loaded the jugs onto
the cart. They sat on the shady rock while
Sylvie tugged the cart to get going.

"Good-bye, little donkey," they called.

Sylvie started up the path alone.

17

The heavy cart dipped and tipped. It got stuck in the ruts and the holes of the path. If it hit a big rock, it stopped short.

Sylvie was going slowly along the path when Flora and Marie caught up with her.

"Please help me," said Sylvie. "You push while I pull. We can go faster."

"What is the big rush?" said Marie. "It's too hot to go fast."

Sylvie kept going.

"I need some water," said Flora. "Let me get a quick drink."

Sylvie kept going.

Marie giggled. "Hey, little donkey! Stop! We are thirsty!"

The cart bucked into a rut. Sylvie pulled hard to keep going.

"Little donkey wants to go," said Flora.

Marie giggled again.

Sylvie stopped and stomped her foot. "Little donkey wants to read and write," she said. "I need to go faster. I need to get back to the village before school is over."

Flora and Marie quit teasing. They knew Sylvie was serious. "Let's go!" they said.

Marie helped push. Flora helped steer. Sylvie pulled the cart over the path.

They got back to the village in no time at all, but they were still too late. When the girls passed the school, it was empty.

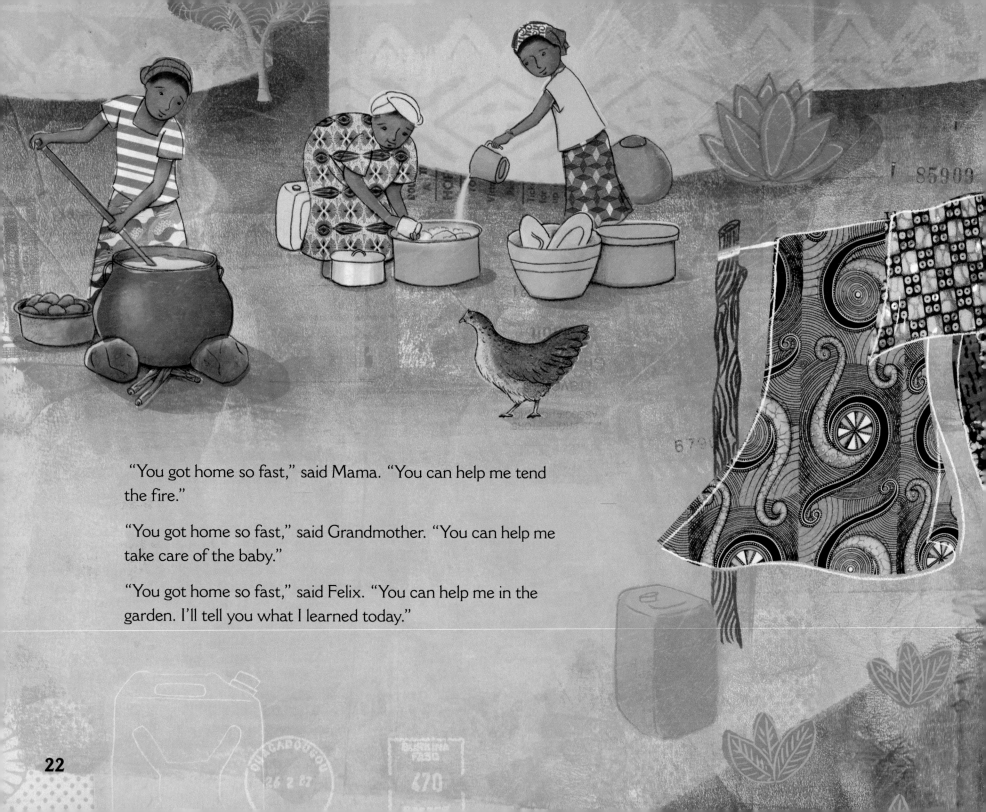

"You got home so fast," said Mama. "You can help me tend the fire."

"You got home so fast," said Grandmother. "You can help me take care of the baby."

"You got home so fast," said Felix. "You can help me in the garden. I'll tell you what I learned today."

Sylvie followed Felix to the garden. She felt tired and sad. The water cart gave her time for more jobs, but it did not give her time for school.

"You should feel proud of your job," said Felix. "You help all of us. We cannot live without water. Today, my teacher said that a seven-year-old boy like me needs to drink almost two liters of clean, fresh water each day to stay healthy. We depend on the work you do, Sylvie."

"I know," said Sylvie. "I do feel proud. I just wish I could go to school, too." Sylvie felt in her heart that reading and writing were important. What if she could grow up to be a doctor or a teacher? Then she could help her family and a lot of other people, too.

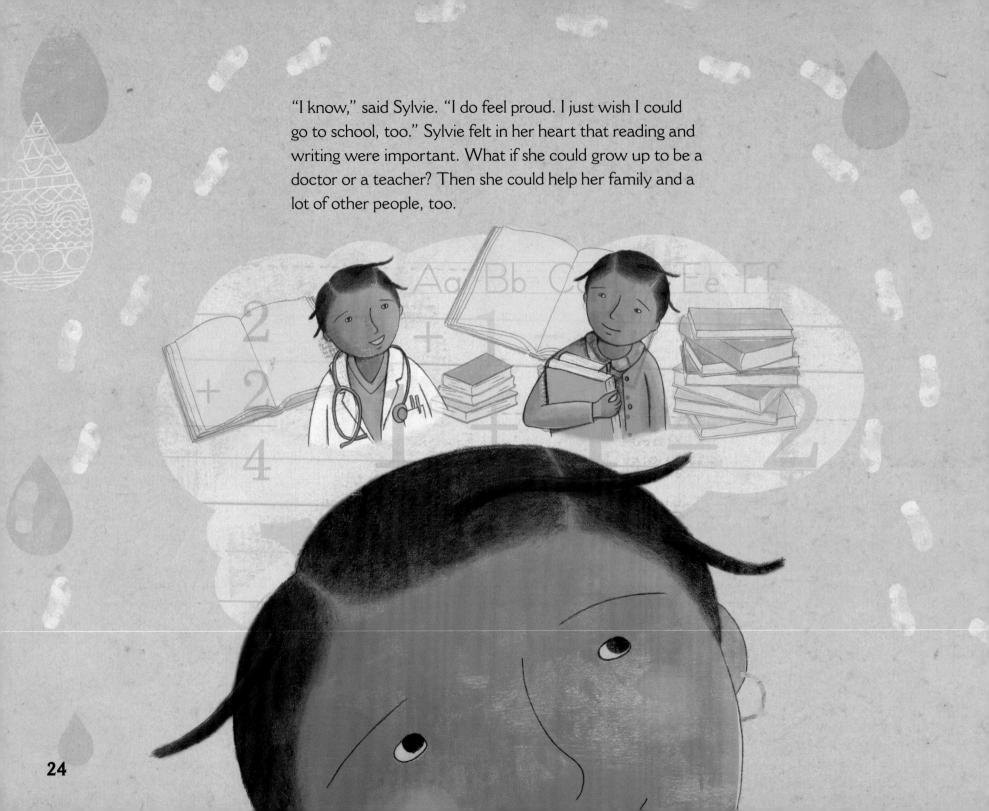

Felix felt bad for Sylvie. He tried to cheer her up. "Do you want to hear today's fun fact?"

Sylvie nodded.

"There are 20,000 drops of water in a liter," said Felix.

"And that is how many steps I must take with my little legs to get to the river and back," said Sylvie. "That is one step for every drop."

A few weeks later, Jean came home with news. He had been to the marketplace in a nearby village. The village had a well.

"A pipe comes up out of a deep hole in the ground," said Jean. "The pipe is in the middle of the village. The families can get as much water as they need."

Flora and Marie burst out laughing. "You are joking," said Flora. "Water out of a pipe? Don't tease."

"He's not teasing," said Felix. "We learned about wells in school. There can be huge lakes and rivers right under our feet."

The sisters laughed even harder. But Sylvie felt excited. "Can our village get a well?" she asked.

"That is the best part," said Jean. "I spoke with Mr. Mike. He says our village has already been chosen for a Water Project. Work will begin very soon."

Sylvie could hardly wait! Every day as she pulled the cart around the final bend in the path, she hoped she'd see the well-building crew. Every night she prayed for the crew to come.

And finally it happened! One day, Sylvie and her sisters came home to find a crew with a big, tall machine set up near the village. It was a drilling rig. It was used to dig a deep, deep hole.

All the families in the village gathered at the well site. Jean and Mr. Mike helped the crew set everything in place. Then they moved aside and asked Sylvie to step forward.

Sylvie smiled. She wrapped her hand around the pump handle. It felt like the handle of the water cart. She thought of all the steps she had taken to bring water to her family, drop by drop. Then she pumped the handle up and down. Clean, fresh water flowed out of the pipe.

Everyone was so happy!

But no one was happier than Sylvie, who finally got to go to school.

When Mike finished the story, I started thinking. Everyone needs water. People can't do anything without it. Water makes things happen.

I asked Sister Mary Jerome to help me do some research. What could we do to support a Water Project?

I found out that it costs about $10,000 to build a well. That's a lot of money. No wonder people like Sylvie have to wait.

Every morning we pray for Sylvie and her family. Thinking about her story gave me an idea. Now my class is raising money to help pay for a well! We made fancy plastic pins in the shape of water drops for people to wear. We are selling them at the art fair and at the farmers' market. It is a cool way to earn money to send to Catholic Relief Services while we spread the word about the importance of clean water. My friends and I are glad we can help make a difference to girls like Sylvie, drop by drop!

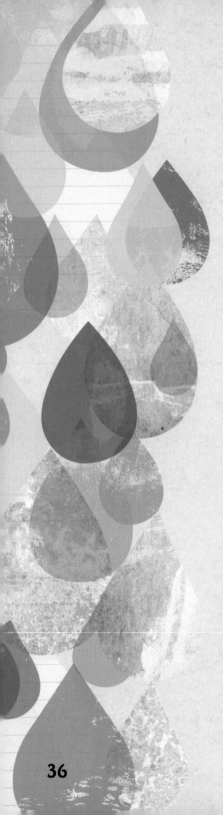

We Need Clean Water

Most communities in the United States have clean water, so it is easy to forget that water is one of our most important resources. Why is having clean water so important? In 2014, experts presented the following facts:

- Worldwide, one in nine people do not have clean, safe drinking water.

- In poor countries, over half the schools do not have bathrooms.

- People can get diarrhea when they don't have clean water and bathrooms. Each day, 2,000 children under five years old die from diarrhea.

- Because of water-related illnesses, children around the world miss 443 million days of school every year.

- Half the people in hospitals today are there because of a water-related disease.

Catholics Confront Global Poverty

The United States Conference of Catholic Bishops and Catholic Relief Services work together to help Catholics fight poverty around the world. Overseas, Catholic Relief Services represents Catholics in the United States by helping people—when they are sick, when they are poor, when they go through a disaster, or when they can't meet their basic needs. Clean, safe water is a basic need, and CRS helps bring it to people who need it most.

- Each year, Catholic Relief Services helps provide clean water and bathrooms to over a million people.

- In Bolivia, CRS workers built toilets in the jungles and in the hills so that people would no longer get sick from using unclean water.

- In Africa, Catholic Relief Services dug canals so that farmers could get water to their crops.

- After flooding in the Philippines, Catholic Relief Services helped people purify their water to make it safe to drink.

In the United States, Catholics pray, learn, act, and give to fight poverty around the world through an initiative called Catholics Confront Global Poverty. You can get involved too!

Talk About It

After reading the book, discuss the following questions:

1. How did Sylvie's task of carrying water from the river help her family? What did Sylvie have to give up in order to help?

2. How might you feel if you had to carry water every day rather than go to school? Why?

3. Was the water cart a good solution? Whom did it help? Was there a better solution? Whom did it help?

4. Many of God's children around the world don't have easy access to water or can't go to school. Do you think it's important to help change this? Why?

5. The schoolchildren sold handmade pins to help raise funds to build a well. What might you and your family, friends, or classmates do to help fight poverty?

Possible Answers

1. She brought fresh water to her family for drinking, cooking, and bathing. She had to give up going to school.

2. I would feel afraid. I would feel this way because I know that getting an education is important for my future.

3. The water cart helped make Sylvie's job easier, but she still couldn't go to school. The well was a better solution because Sylvie and other girls could go to school.

4. I think it's important to help those in need because all of God's children have the right to live a safe, healthy life and to go to school.

5. Answers will vary.

Put Two Feet of Love in Action

SOCIAL JUSTICE   CHARITABLE WORKS

Each storybook includes discussion questions and blackline masters for catechists, teachers, and parents to help share the following teachings of the Church in ways that children can readily understand:

- We are called to practice **social justice** and work for foundational change.

- We are called to perform **charitable works** and help others in need.

Visit **www.loyolapress.com/twofeetoflove** to access these teaching materials.

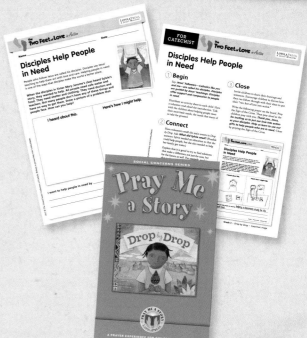

Additionally, a Pray Me a Story reflection guide is available. This guide uses the book as a springboard for entering into imaginative prayer. After hearing the story, the child is gently guided into the scene to meet Jesus and prayerfully speak to him as one friend speaks to another.

The Two Feet of Love *in Action*

SOCIAL JUSTICE

CHARITABLE WORKS

As disciples of Jesus, we must put two feet of love in action!

We walk with the Charitable Works "foot" when we help families meet their needs now, such as giving Sylvie a water cart so she can carry water home more easily.

We walk with the Social Justice "foot" when we help entire communities solve problems permanently, such as helping Sylvie's community build a well so that no one has to walk far away to get water and all the children can go to school.

How can you put two feet of love in action?

Visit the website of the U.S. Catholic bishops for more on the Two Feet of Love in Action.

www.usccb.org/twofeet